for

Cameron

LITTLE TIGER PRESS
An imprint of Magi Publications
23 Manchester Street, London W1M 5PG, UK
First published in Great Britain 1999
Copyright © 1999 Amanda Leslie
Amanda Leslie has asserted her rights to be identified
as the author and illustrator of this work under the
Copyright, Designs and Patents Act, 1988
Printed in Malaysia   ISBN 1 85430 005 6
3 5 7 9 10 8 6 4

Amanda Leslie

flappy waggy wiggly

LITTLE TIGER PRESS
London

woof!

who h
wag
yello
and a
licky

a s a

g y

w tail

sticky

tongue?

dog

who h

wri

green

and

of t

as a

kly

body

a lot

eeth?

odile

snap!

who a w
a w
grey
and
flappy

trumpet!

has
avy
trunk
big
ears?

who's
fluffy,
tail fe
and
quacky

has

blue

athers

a

beak?

oink!

who h
snuf
pink
an
curly
ta

as a
fly
snout
d a
whirly
il ?

who h
long
tongue
spe
slit
bo

as a

red

and a

tty

hery

dy?

grrrowll!

who h
str
orang
and
whis

as a

ipy

e tail

big

kers?.

ti

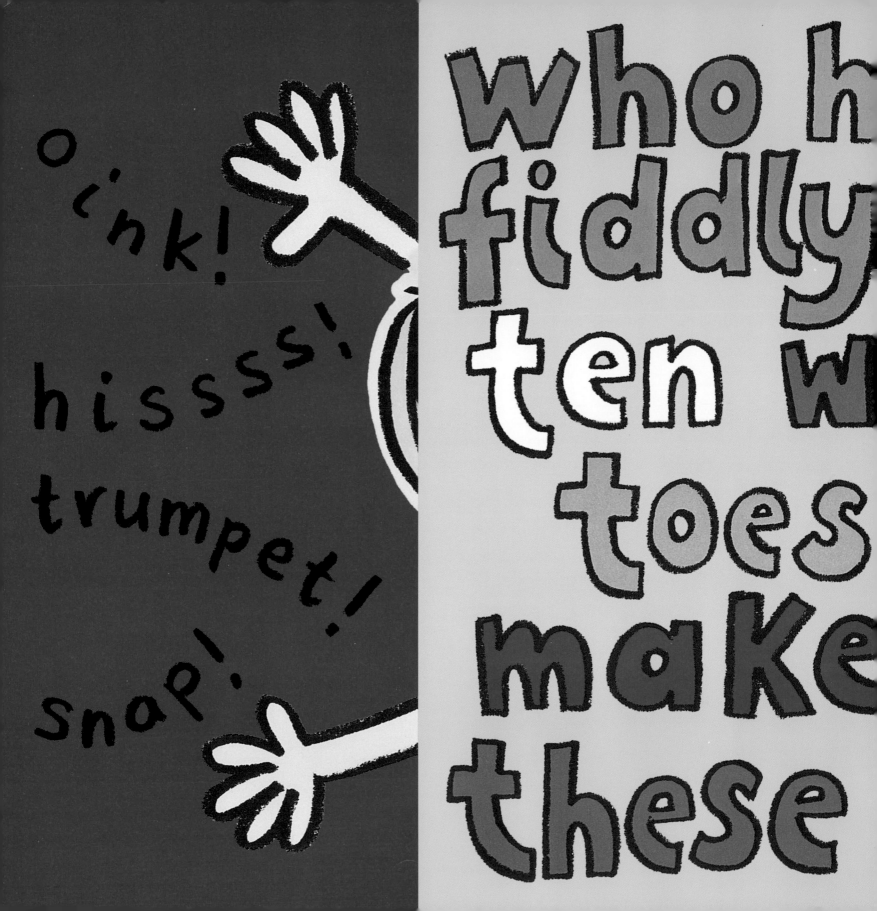

as ten
fingers
iggly
and
s all
noises?